# Welcome to the web-tastic world of...

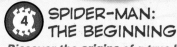

**4** SPIDER-MAN: THE BEGINNING
*Discover the origins of a true hero!*

**5** ADVENTURE STORY: GREEN DEATH BENEATH THE DESERT!
*Spidey faces up to the Green Goblin and the Hulk in this thrilling story!*

**15** FELON FILE # 1: THE GREEN GOBLIN

**16** SPIDER-MAN AND HIS AMAZING POWERS!
*We reveal all of Spidey's secret super-powers!*

**18** SUPER HERO OR SUPER VILLAIN?
*Take this quiz to discover which Spider-Man character you most resemble!*

**31** FELON FILE # 2: THE INCREDIBLE HULK

**32** ESCAPE FROM OSCORP!
*Rescue Spider-Man from the clutches of the Green Goblin!*

**34** WEB OF COLOUR
*Grab your pens and crayons and bring this spider-scene to life!*

**36** ADVENTURE STORY: HUNTER AND HUNTED!
*Kraven the Hunter has Spider-Man in his sights!*

**47** FELON FILE # 3: KRAVEN THE HUNTER

**48** SPIDER-MAN'S WEB OF PUZZLES
*Sink your spider-fangs into these taxing puzzles!*

**61** FELON FILE # 4: CHAMELEON

**62** ANSWERS!

## SPOT THE SPIDER!

As you read through this annual keep an eye out for the **radioactive spider** that gave Peter Parker his powers. Find him *10* times!

£6.99

# SPIDER-MAN
## The Beginning...

Science *expert* but social *outcast*, **Peter Parker** lived with his loving Aunt May and Uncle Ben in a small home in Forest Hills, New York. Peter was like any other teenager, until the day he was bitten by a *radioactive spider...*

The bite gave Peter amazing spider-like **powers**. He could climb up walls and leap across buildings, and his strength and speed had grown to super-human levels!

**UNCLE BEN!!**

Peter decided to use his fantastic powers to get into **show business**. He designed a costume and web-shooters, and wowed audiences everywhere with his **Spider-Man** act!

One night, when Peter was leaving the show, a **burglar** dashed passed him, pursued by a security guard. Despite his powers, Peter didn't stop the burglar — he figured it wasn't his problem.

On getting home, Peter was shocked to discover his Uncle Ben had been *murdered*. Peter caught the killer and only then did he get a good look at his face... It was the very same **burglar** who he could have stopped at the TV studio.

It was then that Peter realised he had been given his powers for a **reason**. Never again would Spider-Man neglect his **duty** to protect the innocent and uphold justice...

*For with great power, comes great responsibility.*

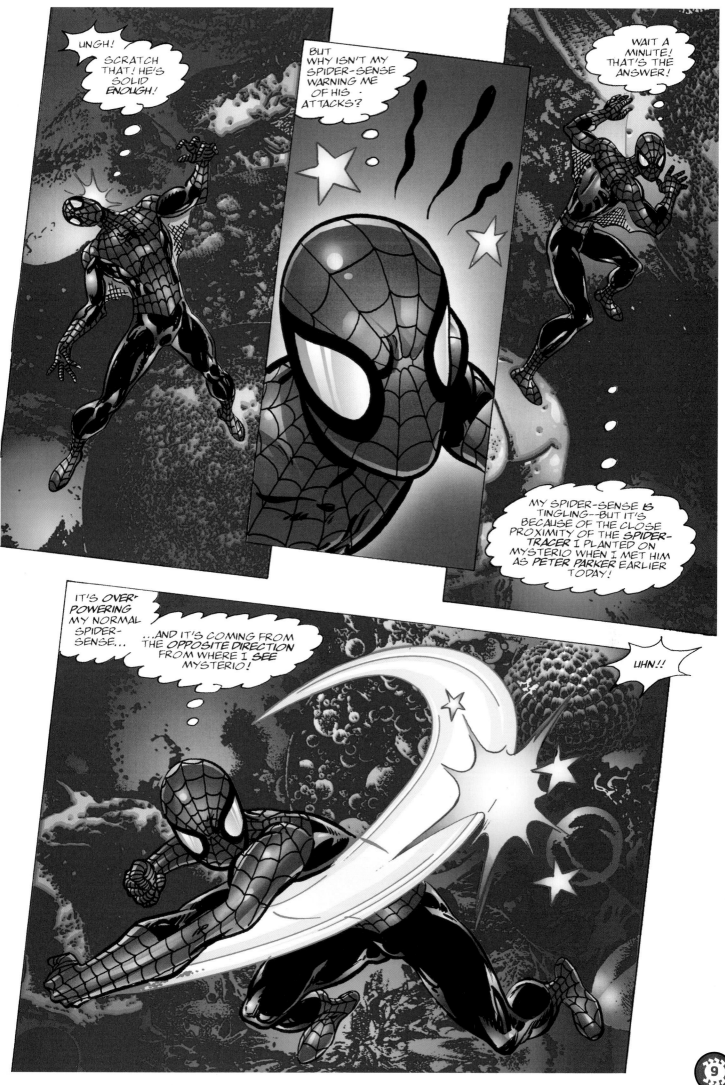

IT'S SUCH A *LONG* WAY TO GO, FOR A BOY OF YOUR TENDER YEARS!

I'M *SEVENTEEN*, AUNT MAY! I'M NOT A *KID* ANY MORE!

AND, ANYWAY, I'LL BE GOING OFF TO *COLLEGE* SOON--THIS WILL BE GOOD PRACTICE, TO SEE IF I CAN *SURVIVE* WITHOUT YOU!

YOU ALWAYS SAY THE RIGHT THING, PETER!

ALL RIGHT--GO AND TAKE THE PICTURES FOR MR. JAMESON. BUT YOU KEEP IN TOUCH!

I'LL TAKE MY *LAPTOP* AND *E-MAIL* YOU EVERY DAY! I PROMISE!

"AND I'LL BE *BACK* BEFORE YOU KNOW IT!"

WOW! I'LL ADMIT I KNOW NEXT TO NOTHING ABOUT MAKING MOVIES--BUT IS THAT *REALLY* ALL THE EQUIPMENT YOU NEED?

AND--WHEN DO I SEE A *SCRIPT*?

WE DON'T NEED A *SCRIPT* FOR THIS PART, SPIDEY.

JUST GO RUN AROUND AND *REACT* TO WHATEVER HAPPENS!

CONTINUED ON PAGE 19...

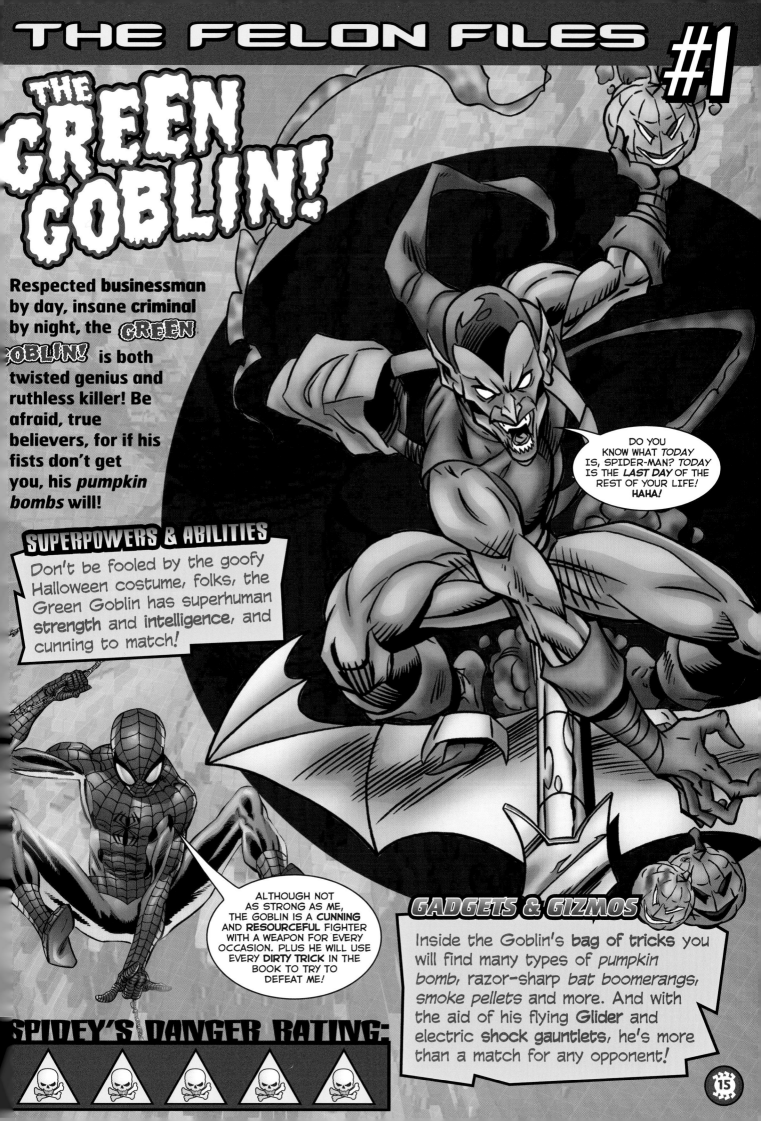

# THE GREEN GOBLIN!

Respected businessman by day, insane criminal by night, the **GREEN GOBLIN!** is both twisted genius and ruthless killer! Be afraid, true believers, for if his fists don't get you, his *pumpkin bombs* will!

## SUPERPOWERS & ABILITIES

Don't be fooled by the goofy Halloween costume, folks, the Green Goblin has superhuman strength and intelligence, and cunning to match!

## SPIDEY'S DANGER RATING:

## GADGETS & GIZMOS

Inside the Goblin's **bag of tricks** you will find many types of *pumpkin bomb*, razor-sharp *bat boomerangs*, *smoke pellets* and more. And with the aid of his flying **Glider** and electric shock gauntlets, he's more than a match for any opponent!

15

# SPIDER-MAN and his amazing... POWERS!

Peter Parker was just an ordinary teenager, until one fateful day when a bite from a *radioactive spider* changed his life forever! Peter gained the fantastic **powers** that would transform him into the amazing Spider-Man. Read on and discover the **secrets** of Spidey's super-powers!

## SUPER SPIDER-SENSE!

MY SPIDER-SENSE IS TINGLING!

Spider-Man's amazing spider-sense is like an in-built *radar* that warns him of danger! A strange tingling sensation in the back of Spidey's skull tells him which way to move to avoid an attack, and makes it impossible for his enemies to sneak up on him!

## SUPER-HUMAN STRENGTH!

Spider-Man can bend iron bars, smash through walls, and lift nearly 10 tons above his head!

## AMAZING AGILITY!

Spidey can run, jump, dive and swing faster than a circus acrobat, without ever getting out of breath!

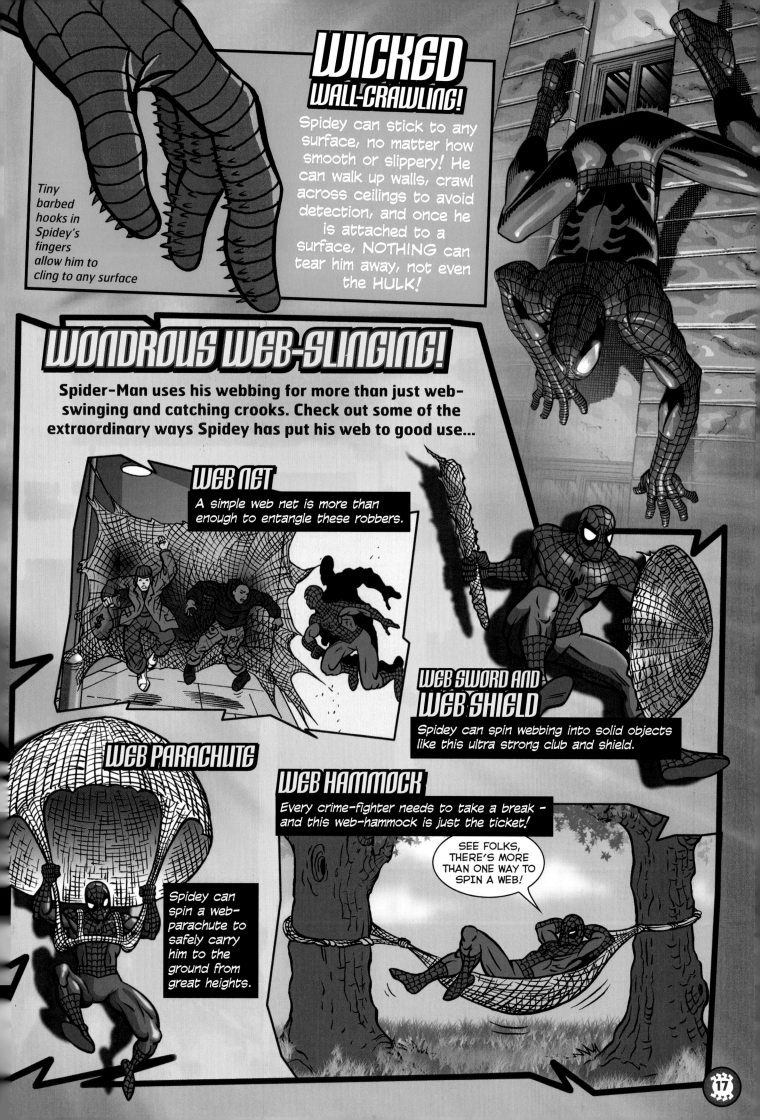

# WICKED
## WALL-CRAWLING!

Spidey can stick to any surface, no matter how smooth or slippery! He can walk up walls, crawl across ceilings to avoid detection, and once he is attached to a surface, NOTHING can tear him away, not even the HULK!

Tiny barbed hooks in Spidey's fingers allow him to cling to any surface

# WONDROUS WEB-SLINGING!

Spider-Man uses his webbing for more than just web-swinging and catching crooks. Check out some of the extraordinary ways Spidey has put his web to good use...

## WEB NET

A simple web net is more than enough to entangle these robbers.

## WEB SWORD AND WEB SHIELD

Spidey can spin webbing into solid objects like this ultra strong club and shield.

## WEB PARACHUTE

Spidey can spin a web-parachute to safely carry him to the ground from great heights.

## WEB HAMMOCK

Every crime-fighter needs to take a break - and this web-hammock is just the ticket!

SEE FOLKS, THERE'S MORE THAN ONE WAY TO SPIN A WEB!

# SUPER HERO or SUPER VILLAIN!

## Take this quiz to discover which Spider-Man character you most resemble!

### START

**Oh no!** The SHOCKER just robbed a bank van! Chasing him yourself could be **dangerous**, but by the time you find a cop, he could be long gone! What do you do?

**FIND A COP**

**MAKE CHASE**

Luckily, you are standing outside a **donut shop** full of cops. You call for help and they give chase. You could lead the charge, but you are kind of peckish...

**JOIN THE CHASE →**

You chase the villain into an alley, with **cop sirens** blaring in the distance. Do you **stall** him until enough cops arrive, or **fight** him on your own?

**EAT SOME DONUTS**

**FIGHT**

**WAIT FOR THE COPS**

The cops arrive, and ask you if this guy was the robber. If you say yes, the Shocker goes to jail. But If you say no, maybe he will share his booty with you? What do you do?

The police take the Shocker to jail. But hey, where's your *reward*? Do you demand payment for your help, or just walk away, happy that justice has been done?

**SAY YES**

### GREEN GOBLIN!
The Shocker escapes, but when you ask him to share his loot, he laughs in your face! Like the **Green Goblin**, you are only out for yourself!

**DEMAND MONEY**

**WALK AWAY**

**SAY NO →**

### HULK!
The Shocker knocks you down and escapes before the police arrive. Like **Hulk**, you have rushed in without *thinking* about your actions! Courage is important, but so is **brains**!

### SPIDER-MAN!
You used your brains *and* your courage to save the day! And for you, **justice** is your only reward, just like **Spider-Man**!

### SILVER SABLE!
Like the mercenary **Silver Sable**, you are brave and resourceful, but you shouldn't always expect a reward for doing good deeds!

### KINGPIN!
The cops didn't catch the Shocker, and to cap it all, you nicked their donuts too! With no respect for the law (and a full belly), you are most like the **Kingpin**!

...CONTINUED FROM PAGE 14

THAT'S WHY! A MILITARY HELICOPTER. THEY MUST BE *HUNTING* FOR THE HULK.

YEAH--I'LL BET THAT LITTLE CAVE-IN CAUSED SEISMOGRAPHS TO JUMP ALL OVER THE PLACE, AND THE AIR FORCE WOULD CHECK IT OUT, IN CASE IT WAS OL' GREENSKIN!

BUT... WHERE THE HECK IS THE CAMERA CREW? DON'T TELL ME THEY DUCKED OUT AND DIDN'T GET *ANY* FOOTAGE..??

AH, WELL! THAT'S NOT *MY* PROBLEM, IS IT? I'LL DRAG MY BUTT BACK TO TOWN AND REMIND OSBORN HE STILL OWES ME *HALF A MILLION* DOLLARS!

"ON THE CONTRARY, SPIDER-MAN."

PERHAPS YOU SHOULD HAVE *READ* THAT CONTRACT, BEFORE YOU SIGNED IT.

I DON'T HAVE TO PAY YOU ANYTHING UNTIL *COMPLETION* OF THE FILM--AND AS OF NOW, COMPLETION SEEMS *MOST* UNLIKELY!

OH, FOR...

ALL RIGHT, OSBORN--YOU GOT ME ON A *TECHNICALITY!*

OBVIOUSLY IT'D BE *TOUGH* FOR *SPIDER-MAN* TO *SUE* ANYBODY!

"BUT AT LEAST I DON'T HAVE TO DEPEND ON YOU FOR A RIDE HOME!"

I'M SORRY, MR. PARKER. MR. JAMESON *CANCELED* YOUR RETURN TICKET. HE LEFT A *MESSAGE* SAYING YOU COULD PICK UP YOUR *BUS* TICKET OVER THERE...

BUS..?

DRAT! I NEVER SHOULD HAVE TOLD HIM I DIDN'T GET ANY PICTURES *BEFORE* I GOT BACK TO NEW YORK!

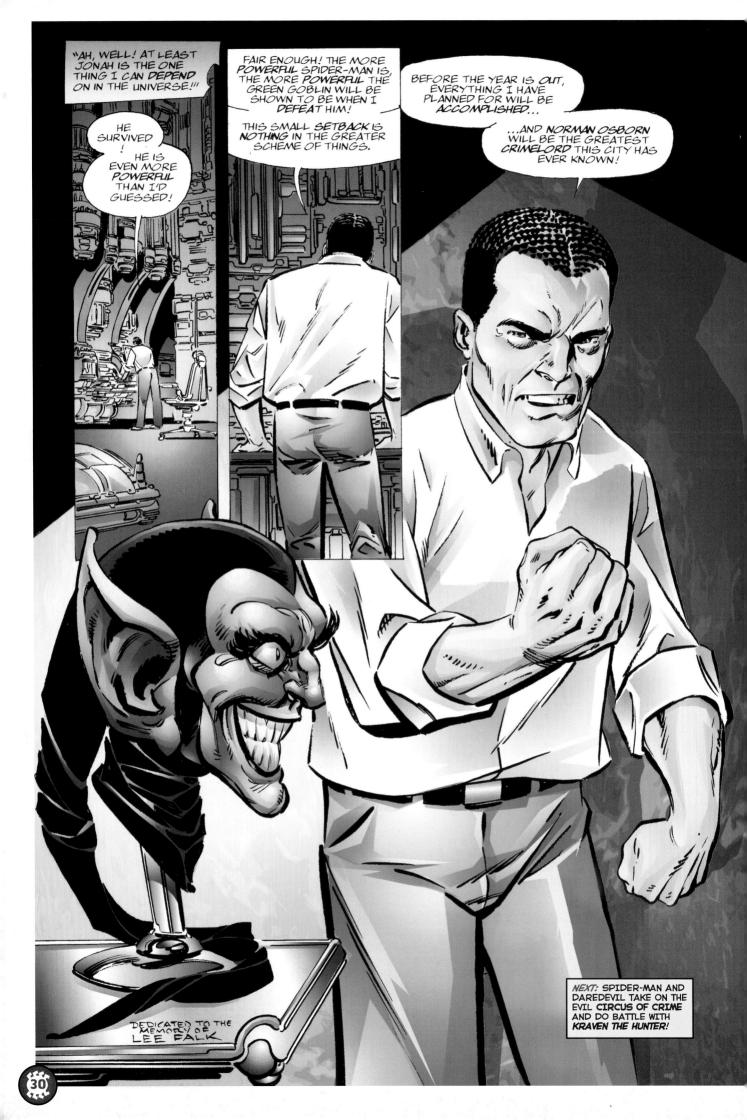

# ESCAPE FROM OSCORP!

**START →**

Oh boy! Spidey has been captured by the GREEN GOBLIN, and imprisoned on the roof of Osborn Chemical! Enter the building and make your way up to the roof to rescue Spidey, avoiding all the dangers on the way!

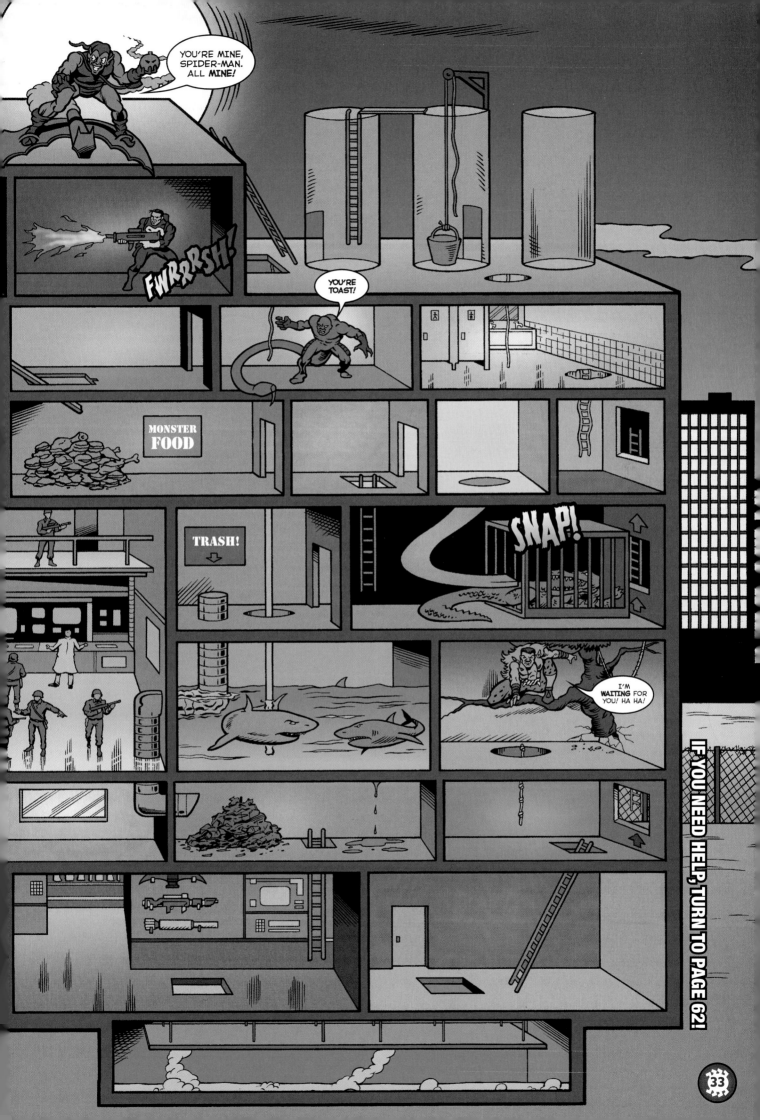

IF YOU NEED HELP, TURN TO PAGE 62!

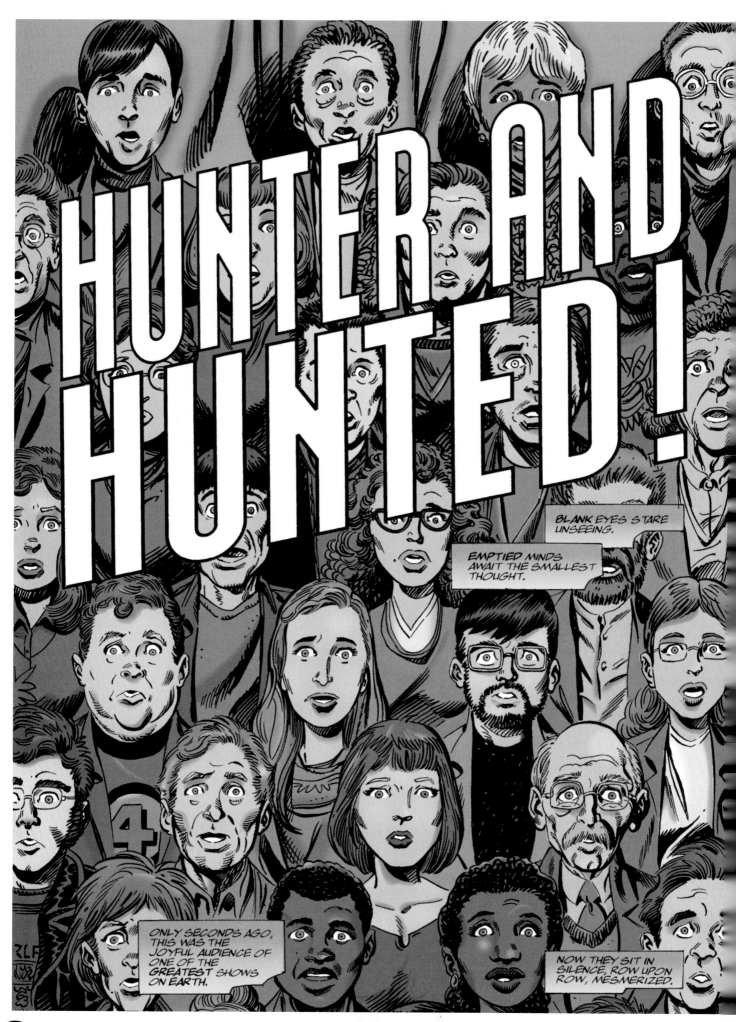

MUST... OBEY... RINGMASTER!

THUD!

HIS STRENGTH IS INCREDIBLE! SO MUCH GREATER THAN A NORMAL MAN!

WAIT! HE'S STOPPING..?

SPIDER-MAN! DON'T JUST STAND THERE! FINISH HIM!!

AND SINCE I HAPPEN TO BE A NORMAL MAN, AT LEAST IN THAT DEPARTMENT...

OF COURSE! SPIDER-MAN HAS NO WILL, NO MIND OF HIS OWN!

HE CANNOT ACT UNLESS THE RINGMASTER COMMANDS IT!

CONTINUED ON PAGE 50...

# KRAVEN THE HUNTER!

In the deepest jungles, a terrifying figure stalks his prey. Clad in camouflaged animal skins, and armed with **deadly poison-tipped blades**, behold **Kraven**, greatest hunter that ever lived!

**I HAVE SPACE FOR ONE MORE HUNTING TROPHY ON MY WALL... IT SHALL BE THE HEAD OF SPIDER-MAN, HAHAHA!**

## SUPERPOWERS & ABILITIES

A witch doctor gave Kraven a special **potion** that made him *stronger than a bear*, and *faster than a cheetah!* Plus, Kraven's hunting and tracking skills are unrivalled; no creature is safe!

**KRAVEN IS A MASTER HUNTER, AND WOULD ALWAYS TRY TO LURE ME INTO A TRAP. I WOULD HAVE TO USE MY SPIDER-SPEED TO AVOID HIS POISON TIPPED BLADES, AND MY WEBBING TO TIE HIM UP.**

## GADGETS & GIZMOS

The horns on Kraven's belt contain **poisons** and toxins he uses against his prey. He also carries **spears, knives, nets** and other hunting devices.

## SPIDEY'S DANGER RATING:

# Spider-Man's...
# WEB OF PUZZLES!

*HEY SPIDER-FANS! GRAB A WEB CORD AND SWING YOUR WAY INTO THESE WEB-TASTIC PUZZLES AND GAMES!*

## CAUGHT ON CAMERA!

Check out these two photos of Spider-Man in battle with his archenemies, and try and spot **8** differences between them!

*HERE'S A CHALLENGE, WEB-FANS... CAN YOU NAME EVERY CHARACTER IN THIS PICTURE?*

## SPIDEY BRAIN BUSTER!

Prove your superhero supremacy by solving these clues and writing the answers in the word grid below!

### ACROSS

1. When he's angry, Bruce Banner turns into the Incredible-
3. Carnage is the colour-
5. Norman Osborn is better known as the Green -
7. Peter Parker's girlfriend is called Mary-
9. He is the greatest hunter of them all!

### DOWN

2. This overweight mob boss runs all the crime in New York!
3. This grey villain uses his horn to smash through walls!
6. This reptilian rogue is actually Dr Curt Connors
8. Spidey shoots this from his wrists

*FOR A BONUS POINT, TAKE EACH LETTER INSIDE A **YELLOW** SQUARE AND RE-ARRANGE THEM TO SPE ONE OF MY **SUPER HERO** FRIENDS!*

MY SUPER HERO FRIEND IS...

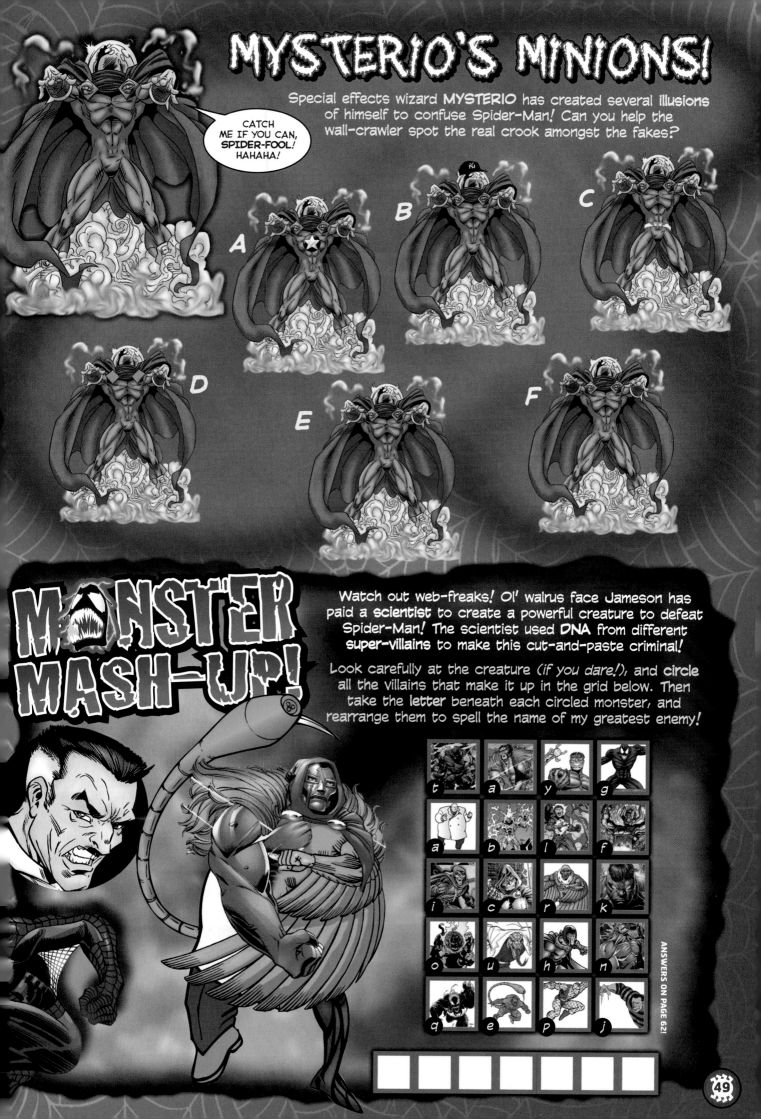

# MYSTERIO'S MINIONS!

Special effects wizard **MYSTERIO** has created several illusions of himself to confuse Spider-Man! Can you help the wall-crawler spot the real crook amongst the fakes?

CATCH ME IF YOU CAN, SPIDER-FOOL! HAHAHA!

A  B  C  D  E  F

# MONSTER MASH-UP!

Watch out web-freaks! Ol' walrus face Jameson has paid a scientist to create a powerful creature to defeat Spider-Man! The scientist used **DNA** from different super-villains to make this cut-and-paste criminal!

Look carefully at the creature (*if you dare!*), and circle all the villains that make it up in the grid below. Then take the **letter** beneath each circled monster, and rearrange them to spell the name of my greatest enemy!

t  a  y  g
a  b  l  f
i  c  r  k
o  u  h  n
q  e  p  j

ANSWERS ON PAGE 62!

49

"I AM HERE TO HUNT SPIDER-MAN!"

I DON'T CARE IF IT'S LEGAL OR NOT! IF YOU WERE THERE, PARKER, WHY DIDN'T YOU GET PICTURES??

I'M NOT SURE WE WANT PICTURES OF A PUBLICITY HOUND LIKE THIS KRAVEN GUY, JONAH.

WHY PLAY HIS GAME?

YEAH--EVERYBODY KNOWS YOU HATE SPIDER-MAN, J.J...

...BUT NOT ENOUGH TO ENDORSE THIS NUTBALL, SURELY?

KID, I'D ENDORSE DOCTOR DOOM FOR PRESIDENT, IF I THOUGHT IT WOULD SELL ONE MORE PAPER!

NOW GET OUT OF HERE! YOU HAVE YOUR ASSIGNMENT! I WANT PICTURES OF KRAVEN CAPTURING SPIDER-MAN!

BE THERE WHEN IT HAPPENS!

OH--BELIEVE ME, JONAH...

"...IF IT HAPPENS, YOU CAN BET I'LL BE THERE!"

YOU WERE RIGHT, MY FRIEND! SPIDER-MAN IS, INDEED, A PRIZE WORTHY OF MY SKILLS!

JUST DON'T LOSE SIGHT OF THE REAL GOAL HERE, KRAVEN.

YOUR SPORT IS A SECONDARY CONSIDERATION.

I WANT MY REVENGE ON SPIDER-MAN!

AND YOU SHALL HAVE IT, CHAMELEON, BEFORE THE WEEK IS OUT!

A DAY LATER, AS PETER PARKER SEEKS THE COMFORT OF HIS DAILY ROUTINE...

MY HANDS DIDN'T STOP SHAKING ALL NIGHT!

IS IT SOME LEFTOVER EFFECT OF KRAVEN'S VENOM, OR AM I REALLY LOSING MY NERVE?

HE DID SHAKE ME UP PRETTY BAD!

OH, NO!

PARKER! WHAT THE DEVIL ARE YOU PLAYING AT??

THIS IS THE LAST SORT OF BEHAVIOR I WOULD EXPECT FROM YOU, PARKER!

NOW, CLEAN UP THIS MESS AT ONCE!

Y-YESSIR...

HAW HAW! LOOKS LIKE TEACHER'S PET HAS FINALLY LOST HIS MAGIC TOUCH!

BUT THE DAY IS NOT YET DONE WITH PETER.

AS HE WANDERS HOME FROM MIDTOWN HIGH...

OH, NO! LOOKS LIKE JONAH MADE SOME KIND OF CONNECTION WITH KRAVEN AFTER ALL!

Daily Bugle
DEFEAT OF SPIDER-MAN IMMINENT SAYS KRAVEN

WHAT HAVE THOSE TWO GOT COOKED UP FOR ME?

AND, LATER THAT EVENING...

I'VE READ UP EVERYTHING I CAN FIND ON KRAVEN. IF THIS GUY IS EVEN HALF HIS REPUTATION, I MAY BE IN SERIOUS TROUBLE!

BUT WHAT HAPPENS TO AUNT MAY IF...

PETER, DEAR, ARE YOU STILL STUDYING?

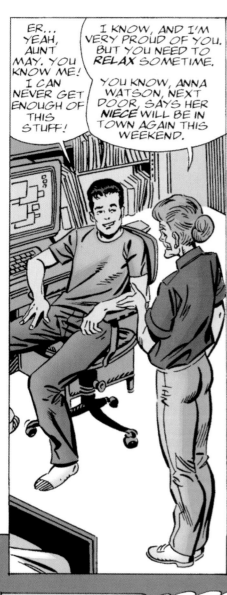

ER... YEAH, AUNT MAY. YOU KNOW ME! I CAN NEVER GET ENOUGH OF THIS STUFF!

I KNOW, AND I'M VERY PROUD OF YOU. BUT YOU NEED TO RELAX SOMETIME.

YOU KNOW, ANNA WATSON, NEXT DOOR, SAYS HER NIECE WILL BE IN TOWN AGAIN THIS WEEKEND.

I KNOW YOU'RE YOUNG STILL, AND YOU HAVE COLLEGE TO THINK ABOUT...

...BUT FROM THE WAY ANNA DESCRIBES THIS GIRL SHE SOUNDS LIKE SHE WOULD BE PERFECT FOR YOU--VERY QUIET AND STUDIOUS.

I'VE TOLD ANNA YOU'D LOVE TO TAKE HER OUT ON A DATE THIS FRIDAY NIGHT.

A BLIND DATE? OH, GREAT! THAT'S ALL I NEED RIGHT NOW!

ER... THANKS, AUNT MAY. IF I HAVE THE TIME, I'LL...

NO "IFS," PETER. THIS IS ALL SETTLED. FRIDAY NIGHT YOU CAN GO TO A MOVIE WITH MARY JANE WATSON.

"YES, AUNT MAY."

MY HANDS ARE SHAKING SO BADLY I CAN'T EVEN SHOOT MY WEBLINES STRAIGHT!

HOW AM I GONNA STOP KRAVEN LIKE THIS?

I'LL HAVE TO GET BY LEAPING FROM BUILDING TO BUILDING.

LUCKY MY SPIDER-ABILITIES DON'T SEEM DIMINISHED BY WHATEVER KRAVEN DID TO ME!

THE END.

BASED ON ORIGINAL WORKS BY STAN LEE AND STEVE DITKO

JOHN AND AL BYRNE MILGROM WRITER-ARTISTS

MARK AND MARK McNABB BERNARDO COLORISTS

RALPH MACCHIO EDITOR

BOB HARRAS EDITOR IN CHIEF

# ANSWERS!

Hey! I hope you're not **CHEATING!** Only look at this page when you think you've solved **ALL THE PUZZLES** in this annual!

## 48 CAUGHT ON CAMERA!

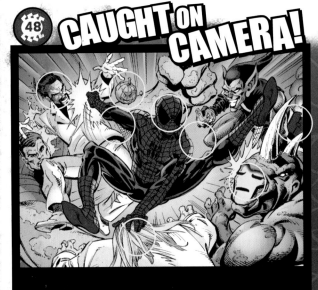

The eight differences have been circled in yellow.

## SPIDEY BRAIN BUSTER!

The answers have been filled in for you on the word grid.

The letters in the yellow boxes combine to spell DAREDEVIL, Spidey's superhero friend!

```
¹HULK
    I
    N
    G   ³RED
   ⁵GOBLIN  H
    I    I  I
    P    Z  N
⁷JANE     A  O
         R  ⁸W
        ⁹KRAVEN
             E
             B
```

## MYSTERIO'S MINIONS!

The real Mysterio is E!

CURSES! YOU OUTWITTED ME!

## MONSTER MASH-UP!

The evil cloned monster is made up of the following Spidey villains:

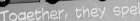

Together, they spell

## 32 ESCAPE FROM OSCORP!

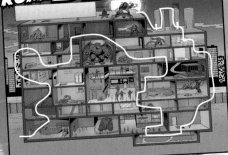

The safe route through the Oscorp building to Spider-Man on the roof has been marked on the maze below in white.

THAT'S ALL FOR NOW FOLKS! UNTIL NEXT TIME, KEEP ON SWINGIN'!

## 34 WEB OF COLOUR!

The 10 pumpkin bombs have been circled in green. The 10 bats have been circled in blue.

## 62

The 10 spiders can be found on pages 4, 8, 16, 20, 32, 35, 40, 47, 48 and 52